LITTLE SAMMY GREEN
LOVES FRIED GREEN APPLES

by **Kellie Rowel** and **Keith A. Rowel**

with contributions from Dr. Randolph Rowel, Kye Rowel, Toni Whitehead and Chelsea Rowel

PALMETTO
PUBLISHING

First Edition

Hardcover ISBN: 978-1-68515-106-5
Paperback ISBN: 978-1-63837-024-6

DEDICATION

This book is dedicated
to all our ancestors "who toiled hard
so that the next generations could afford to
be free thinkers"?

TUBMAN TRIBUTE
FROM: COUSIN SAMMY

Salute to the troops who saved us all.
Salute to the troops who taught us how to crawl. Salute to
the troops who saved us from destruction.

Salute to the troops who showed us freedom and
real life's introduction.
Harriet my queen your bravery saved us,
Harriet my queen I am here, no fear.
Lead the people to my temple and we will set them free.

Your bravery for our people is one of a kind.
I am proud to be your family and stand beside you
as one sound mind!
I, Rev. Samuel Green will show you the way.
You can come to me any time, night or day!
Because of you, we are free and able to live life our own way!

Harriet, my Harriet, you are a true queen, I must say!

Kellie Rowel

The Fried Green Apples children's book series is a family project that includes Keith as the concept artist, his daughters, Kellie as the storywriter and Kye as editor, and 14-year-old granddaughter, Toni "TT," who inspired much of the illustrations, and his brother Randy who penned the Author's Note.

Collectively they've joined to create the fantasy world of Mulberry Hill. A magical fruit farm town of Mulberry Hill off the shores of the Chesapeake Bay. The magical experiences are built around the lives of the Green Family ancestors who herald the message of neighbors helping neighbors. Rev. Samuel Green, who was the first cousin to Harriet Tubman, is depicted as the boy Little Sammy Green who plays in the ravine and loves Fried Green Apples.

One of the morals of this story is that Little Sammy Green listened when his Mama called him to come home. Little Sammy did not question her and neither did he hesitate. He Listened, Obeyed, and Responded to his Mama's call to come home. What a Treat!

Fried Green Apples,
    for me Sammy Green!
I can eat them anytime,
breakfast dinner and
    in between!

I hear mama calling—
Sammy Green!
Sammy Green!
Your Fried Green
Apples are ready!
It's time to be seen!

- 7 -

"I'm Coming Mama,"
I yell,
from deep in the ravine!
Don't eat them without me.
I'm running as fast as my feet
carry me!

The thought of sweet,
ooey-gooey,
delicious, tart treats!
Gets me excited
from my head
to my feet!

"I'm finally here," I yell.
I wash my hands
and take my seat!
The taste
of the sweetness
on my tongue!
What a treat!
What a Treat!

AUTHOR'S NOTE

Years ago, while in a conversation with my wise grandfather. I shared concerns that many of his grandchildren were navigating life by not always making the right decisions. I had asked, "Aren't you worried about how our life might turn out if we continue down this path?" With his head tilted, Rev. Charles A. Green chuckled, and said, "Son when you were born, your grandmother, your parents, and I planted a seed in you as we did in others born after or before you. Now once that seed was planted, you were connected to a cord. We knew that some of you might get lost at times and run on and on in the wrong direction, but sooner than later, that cord would reach its end and you would return to your roots where the seeds were originally planted and redirect you toward the right path. No, we never worried and knew you would come back to your roots because of our faith in God."

This is the basic premise behind the Mulberry Hill book series for children that is keeping the legacy alive by sharing the principles our ancestors learned by, worked by, and lived by. Although the Mulberry Hill stories are fictional, the names and character of those in the stories are real and stem from seven generations of my family, starting with the Rev. Samuel Green, Sr.

Born and enslaved in Dorchester, Maryland, in 1802, Rev. Samuel Green, Sr., became an underground railroad conductor and was instrumental in helping slaves escape to freedom. He was later arrested in 1857 for these acts and for having in his procession Uncle Tom's Cabin, a book that spoke openly about the evils of slavery. During this time of struggle, Rev. Samuel Green, Sr., was not alone. He and Harriet Rit Green (Tubman) were the grandchildren of Modesty Green and therefore first cousins. His legacy continued through his son Rev. Samuel Green, Jr., grandson Oliver Leslie Green, great-grandson, Rev. Charles Green, and now generations of family including the authors of this book series who were called to continue his legacy.

Little Sammy Green and the Fried Green Apples is evidence that we returned to our roots where the seeds were originally planted, seven generations ago. This book series in also consistent with the mission of the Reverend Samuel Green Sr. Foundation Inc., which is to reach out to educate the social, historical, cultural, spiritual, and civil rights needs of the people of our nation, beginning in the state of Maryland.

As a board member of the Reverend Samuel Green Sr. Foundation Inc., I urge you to sit back and know that reading the Mulberry Hill book series for children is a journey filled with stories that highlight the principles that guided these great men and women who understood that "Education is the 21st Century Underground Railroad."

Families Magical Tree House
by Toni "TT" at age 13

A Bicycle in the Tree
by Toni "TT" at age 13

Green Apple Tree Ravine
by Toni "TT" at age 13

Kellie Rowel was born in Annapolis, Maryland in 1982. As a child Kellie was always fun and energetic. Growing up writing was not her first love. However, she always wrote to express her feelings in ways she couldn't verbally. Kellie soon realized that poetry was an outlet for her free thinking. When her dad asked her about writing a Children's book, it was a no brainer for her. Combining her love for children and her love for writing into one was heaven-sent. Now she is giving the world a taste of "Fried Green Apples" mixed with family, love, and history! The books from the *"Fried Green Apples Series"* are written from the heart and with lots of love. We hope that you will always enjoy reading them as much as we enjoyed writing them for your family!

Keith A. Rowel is an innovative person of inspirational morals and values to share throughout the world. While working in an elementary school Keith was inspired with the concept to write a Children's book around the life of his famous 4th generation grandfather Rev. Samuel Green, Sr. who was the 1st cousin to Harriet Rit Green (Tubman), as well he assisted her with freeing slaves through the underground railroad. With this inspiration Keith reached out to his daughter Kellie to write a fictional tale about his family's fruit farm town of Mulberry Hill. In the "Fried Green Apples Series" Mulberry Hill is a magical fruit farm that depicts his great-grandfather as a little boy who played in the ravine. The character of *"Little Sammy Green who loves Fried Green Apples"* was born. It is our hope and desire that everyone who reads our books will enjoy and share these stories for many years to come.

CPSIA information can be obtained
at www.ICGtesting.com
Printed in the USA
BVHW090849300921
617789BV00002B/168